OUT OF THIS WORLD

Written by Fran Pickering
Illustrated by Bob Moulder

HENDERSON
PUBLISHING LTD

It's a strange world out there

We use the word 'supernatural' to describe objects, events, or talents that people have, that seem to be 'outside' or 'extra' to what we consider to be normal or natural.

Usually it just means that we have not, as yet, got a complete understanding of these things. We can't explain how or why they happen, but the fact that they ***do*** happen means that they fall within the laws that operate in our universe – we just don't know all of those laws yet!

So, remember, things often only seem 'weird' or 'spooky' because our minds find it hard to cope with what we can't explain. Here in the West we have been trained from birth to use mainly the left side of our brains. This is the logical, rational thinking bit – we like neat answers and little, labelled boxes to put things in.

So if something happens and it doesn't fit into one of our boxes, we panic and yell 'supernatural', when all we probably need is another box for which we don't yet have the label. Or maybe we need to get rid of all our boxes!

Roaming Romans

In the early 1980s a heating engineer was working in the cellar of the medieval Treasurer's House in York, England, when he heard a trumpet sound close at hand. To his amazement and horror, a man wearing a short skirt and carrying a round shield, marched through the wall of the cellar! Hot on his heels came an officer on horseback and then a line of about sixteen men. The procession marched across the cellar and disappeared through the opposite wall. The men were only visible from their thighs upwards! The only glimpse the engineer had of their lower legs and feet was when they passed through a hole he had dug in the floor. They wore hand dyed kilts of streaky green and leather helmets. He thought they were Roman soldiers, marching along the site of the old Roman road, but when he reported his ghosts he was told that the Romans did not use round shields. Later it was discovered that the Sixth Legion who were based at York had special volunteers, who carried round shields!

Black Dogs

One fairly common phantom in the UK and one also seen in France, is that of a huge black dog, often with red eyes. Usually the dog appears and disappears silently, sometimes vanishing into thin air near water or bridges over water, leaving a strong smell of sulphur behind him. Pooh! They are mostly seen on ancient sites such as old tracks, barrows, old churchyards and places where ley lines are known to run. The dogs look very real and solid, but people who try to hit them with a stick or umbrella find that the object passes right through!

In 1928, a student fishing by a river in County Londonderry, Northern Ireland, looked up to see a large black dog walking along the riverbank towards him. No one else was in sight and the dog was huge, so the student threw down his rod and climbed the nearest tree. As the dog passed below the tree it looked up with fiery red eyes and snarled loudly.

In Scotland, two places are named after the black dog: Caisteal a Choin Dubh (Castle of the black dog), near Craignish, and Dun a Choin Dubh (Fort of the black dog) at Knapdale, and phantom dogs were regular visitors to both.

Ghostly Cities

If you want to see the city of Bristol, UK, go to Alaska! Legend has it that every year between June 21st and July 10th, a ghostly image of Bristol appears in the sky above Alaska. Over the years, even before white people came to Alaska, many people (including Alaskan Indians) have reported seeing quite clearly in the sky "...houses, streets and trees. Here and there rose tall spires over huge buildings, which appeared to be ancient mosques or cathedrals." Most viewers think the image is not of Bristol, but of a much more ancient city.

On 2nd August, 1908, a phantom city appeared for three hours over Ballyconneely, Southern Ireland. In 1796, 1797 and 1801, a walled city was seen in the sky over Youghal, also in Ireland.

In the 1880s a whole string of cities, islands and other scenes kept appearing and disappearing in the skies over Sweden.

On 27th September, 1846, the ghostly image of what locals thought was Edinburgh appeared over Liverpool, England.

Ghostly Portraits

Next time you have a family photograph taken, have a close look at it – you might see someone who wasn't there peering over Grandma's shoulder! One very common form of ghost is one that people never see in real life, but which appears on photographs when they are developed. Many of these films with ghostly images on have been tested by photographic laboratories, but the results were inconclusive. Spooky!

One or two psychiatrists and scientists have carried out experiments in which an image of something that someone was thinking hard about has come out as a fuzzy photograph on a photographic film.

Images of family pets that have died often appear on photographs. A photograph of Lady Hehir and her Irish Wolfhound also shows the head of the wolfhound's friend, a Cairn puppy, which had died six weeks earlier. A photograph of her pet cat taken in 1974 shows the cat looking at the ghostly image of a black kitten.

Haunted Houses

Borley Rectory, in the UK, was claimed to be the 'most haunted house in Britain' until it was burnt to the ground in 1976. However, some say that ghosts still haunt the ruins and the nearby Borley Church. The *Daily Mirror* sent a reporter there in 1929, and on June 10th, the newspaper reported dragging footsteps in empty rooms, a nun who roamed the grounds and an old-fashioned coach drawn by two bay horses with a headless coachman. Legend has it that the nun was eloping with a monk when they were caught red-handed. As a result he was hanged and she was bricked up into a wall. The price of true love!

The mansion that is Bowes Museum, at Barnard Castle, County Durham, houses the beautiful paintings, furniture and objects collected by John Bowes and his wife. They are buried nearby and at night their ghosts are said to walk hand in hand around their beloved museum, gazing at their treasures.

A ghost was said to haunt number 50 Berkeley Square, London. Built in the 1700s, the house was once the home of British Prime Minister, George Canning. After his time it became the scene of dreadful hauntings. No one knows exactly what haunted the house, but bumps, bangs, footsteps and furniture being dragged along the floor were heard. One room seemed to be the most haunted of all and a girl, left alone in there, reputedly went mad and never recovered enough to say what she had seen.

Haunted Houses

A first floor flat in London's Admiralty House is haunted by the ghost of Margaret Reay, whose portrait hangs in the house. She was shot dead in April 1779 as she left the Royal Opera House.

In 1969, the owners of the Haw Branch plantation in Virginia, USA, were sent a portrait of a distant relative. Florence had died while still a young woman. When it arrived, the portrait was painted in grey, white and black: rather odd colours, but nonetheless they hung it over the fireplace in the library, in memory of their distant relation. As the days passed, the owners began to hear a woman's voice in the library, but every time they looked it was empty. After a few months something happened to the picture. The rose in the vase in the painting turned red. The next day the vase was green, and then gradually the painting turned from black and white to glorious full colour. When the painting was completely coloured, the voice was never heard again.

In London, until the council straightened the road, there were quite a few accidents at the corner of St Mark's Road and Cambridge Gardens. Most were said to have been caused by motorists trying to avoid a phantom red double-decker bus which careered around the corner, headlights ablaze, but totally devoid of passengers or driver. Once the road was straightened there were no more reports of the ghostly bus.

In the summer of 1929 a new road was opened in Germany. Within a year, more than 100 cars had crashed on the road, always at the same spot – marker 239. Drivers interviewed said they felt a terrific force seize them and pull them off the road. A local dowser (see page 25) walked along the road with his divining rods. At marker 239 the rods flew out of his hand and across the road. He said that a powerful magnetic current ran under the road at that point. To counteract it he buried a copper box full of star-shaped pieces of copper under the road and the accidents miraculously stopped! A week later the police dug up the box and the first three cars to come along after that were wrecked. Hastily they re-buried the box and it has been there ever since.

Electric!

Human beings have their own mild electrical field around them. This is affected by other electrical fields that they come into contact with, usually in such a mild way that no one ever notices.

Some people, especially teenagers, create such a strong electromagnetic force of their own that it can affect outside objects. This could explain noisy ghosts or 'poltergeists' – ghosts that aren't seen but which can move objects.

The electromagnetic force field around a human being can be photographed by a special method of photography called 'Kirlian' photography. Matthew Manning, a famous healer, once 'blew out' two Kirlian photography machines, each generating 35,000 volts. He did this simply by placing his hand on them and concentrating all the energy he had into them.

One survey of psychics – people with ESP (Extrasensory Perception) abilities – showed that all those surveyed had suffered a severe electric shock before the age of 10.

Scientific experiments with Matthew Manning and other psychics showed that they derived these powers by using an old part of the brain that modern man no longer uses.

Super-Mum

A woman in Harrisburg, Pennsylvania, has claimed that living near a 500 kilovolt power line has given her extra powers. She claims to have super-hearing and the ability to see through solid objects! Fluorescent light bulbs apparently light up when carried into the back yard and plants in the area grow in spiral shapes. Very strange indeed!

Flash Gordons

'Flash Gordons' are people who claim to be able to light up light bulbs just by holding them; to attract metal objects like a magnet; to give an electric shock to someone and to cause electrical machines to break down – just by touching them!

Unbelievable? Well, an electric eel can store electricity and deliver an electric shock of 500 volts. So perhaps 'Flash Gordons' are not just a figment of the imagination! We all build up static electricity in our bodies. You may have heard or felt the 'fizz' of this when you have brushed your hair or taken a shirt off quickly over your head.

Things that go Bump

James Herrmann lived in Long Island, New York. In February 1958 he rang the police because he thought someone was trying to attack him. The trouble was, it wasn't someone visible. Bottles of medicine, aftershave and shampoo were uncapping themselves and pouring their contents over the floor. Items on shelves slid to and fro. Ornaments and vases hurtled through the air smashing against walls and on the floor...but all the police could say was: "Something weird is happening there." Well, how would you explain it?

The house of John Wesley, the famous Methodist preacher, was haunted for two months during 1716 and 1717. No ghost was ever seen, but strange rappings, tappings and bangings were heard, along with footsteps on the stairs and an unseen cradle rocking in the nursery.

In 1721, three famous English men of letters – Dr Samuel Johnson, Oliver Goldsmith and Horace Walpole – decided to join forces to investigate ghostly rappings, scratchings and stone throwing in Cock Lane, London. That must have given them something to write home about!

Now and Then

Dean Dahl of Nebraska Weslyan University, Lincoln, USA, asked his secretary to take a message to a colleague in another building. The date was 3rd October, 1963. As his secretary entered the building she heard music and student voices coming from one of the rooms and turned to go inside.

The first thing that hit her as she walked in was the strong, musty smell. Then she saw a woman in a long, black skirt reaching up to the top shelves of an old music cabinet. Everything was deathly quiet; the students' chatter and music had faded away. She looked out of the window. Madison Street was no longer there! All of the usual buildings had disappeared...she seemed to have unwittingly stepped back into the past. Frightened, she turned and went back into the hall, where, once again, the welcome noise and bustle of her own time surrounded her.

A family on holiday in Australia were driving along a motorway. Hurtling towards them in the opposite direction was a long oval object, resembling a metal cylinder. As it whisked past they saw frightened faces peering out of porthole-like windows and noticed that the 'car' had no wheels and was moving above the road. Could this have been a car from the future?

Step Back in Time

In 1896 there lived a shy, seven year old boy who went to a boarding school. His headmaster was very cruel and often made him cry. One day, the boy ran off after lunch and wandered around the town until he came upon a street that led along the back of the shops. The street ended in a high wall where there was a door.

Going through the door, the boy found himself in an extension of the town: almost a small town in itself, with houses unlike any he had ever seen before. Cautiously he explored and went right inside one house, climbing the stairs to a large empty room at the top. Crossing to the window he gazed out over land that sloped away to a valley, and beyond that he saw undulating tree-covered hills – he recognised none of it. Startled, he made his way back to the world he knew. He never was able to find the door in the wall again.

Twenty one years later, the boy, who was now a soldier fighting in World War I, was sent to the 4th Army Headquarters in France, close to the River Somme. At a loose end one evening, he decided to explore the area, taking his sketch pad with him. As he wandered along, he came to a deserted village called Misery. His hair stood on end when he realised that he was in the very same street he had explored all those years ago as an unhappy little boy!

One house in particular attracted him. He went in and climbed the stairs, and to his amazement, found himself in the large room of long ago, looking out on the same landscape he had seen as a child.

This strange experience has been called a 'time-slip'.

History Lesson

In 1901, Miss Mobberley and Miss Jourdain, school teachers, went on holiday to Paris and visited the Palace of Versailles. Strolling around the magnificent gardens, they appear to have stepped straight into the past!

Wandering along chatting they lost their way and asked two gardeners for directions. The men wore long, greenish coats and three-cornered hats, which seemed rather unusual. Further on they saw another man sitting by a small bandstand, wearing a cloak and a sombrero hat. Neither of them liked the look of him and they hurried past. They crossed a small bridge over a waterfall and came to a house. In front of it sat a woman, sketching. She wore a long, low-cut pink dress of very fine material and a wide, shady hat on top of her mass of fair hair. Next the teachers actually spoke to a footman in old-fashioned clothes, and then saw a complete wedding party. At times when they turned to look back, people they had just passed had disappeared.

Visiting the gardens again, they found them to be completely different: buildings, bridges, pathways, woods...all gone! Looking at history books, they discovered the people they saw had been wearing the clothes worn at the time of Marie Antoinette, Queen of France in the 1700s. Was the woman in the pink dress Marie Antoinette herself? How had they been able to speak to some of these people and ask directions?

Comings and Goings

In 1173, in a field just outside the village of Woolpit, near Bury St Edmunds, UK, two children suddenly appeared. Nothing strange in that – except that they were green, wore clothes made from unknown material and could not speak any recognisable language. The children refused all food offered to them and were close to death before they were eventually given bean plants, which they ate. Later, when they had begun eating a variety of food other than green plants, their green colour faded away! Once they had learnt to speak English they claimed to have come from a land where the sun did not rise and to have suddenly disappeared from there with a loud noise.

In August, 1887, two children appeared from a cave near Banjos, Spain. Their skin was green and their clothes were of an unknown material. They neither spoke nor understood Spanish and their eyes were Oriental in shape. These two children also refused to eat and the boy died. The girl, however, survived until 1892, and when she could finally speak Spanish she claimed that they came from a sunless land where one day a whirlwind had deposited them in the cave!

Air Mail

In July, 1993, Ms Denise Brisson was at home in Eaubonne, near Paris, where she was talking to her brother-in-law on the telephone. Suddenly, she thought she heard a loud thump outside. Rushing into the garden she found the frozen body of a man of about 35 years of age. The man had no identification on him, so his identity remained a mystery. French police thought he may have fallen out of an aircraft, but could not explain how he had become frozen. Nor could they explain the clothes he was wearing and the coins in his pocket. The clothes were old-fashioned and the coins were Russian roubles which had been out of use for years…

1173 was a busy year for strange reports. It went down in history as a year of high solar activity – that is, there were electrical storms over the planet, nuclear-like explosions on the sun, the sky glowed red at night and showers of stones fell in various parts of the world.

Lost Empires

In Utah, Colorado, Arizona and North Mexico, there are many deserted cities: ancient cities built high on the wide shelves of the canyons under the rocky outcrops. Every two miles or so in some canyons there is a perfectly preserved little town, formerly lived in by the Anasazi Indians. The name means 'ancient ones' or 'ancient enemy'. Climbing up and down to their homes by means of finger and toe holds in the rock face, they lived safely and peacefully until around 1200 when they suddenly disappeared.

The cities, built of stone, were large and civilised. The Mesa Verdi had over 300 cities on it, with meeting halls, running water, 5-storey buildings and all the mod cons necessary for the many people who would have lived there.

All these people disappeared at the same time. Those cities that are open for exploration today still have grain in the stores, unrolled sleeping mats, shoes on the floor and food prepared ready for meals: all signs that the folk who lived there were not planning to leave. The area is so dry that the bones from dead bodies would still be there, but the only bones ever found were from 20 bodies burnt in an oven.

Where did the rest go without a trace?

Gone Missing

Like all police forces, the Royal Canadian Mounted Police have many unsolved crimes and missing persons on their books. One such case involves the disappearance in 1930 of a complete community of 1200 people!

In the winter of that year a trapper, Arnold Laurent, noticed a strange lighted object in the sky, moving in the direction of Lake Anjikuni. Later, another trapper, Joe Labelle, entered the village on the shores of Lake Anjikuni and found it completely deserted. The villagers' kayaks were tied up on the lakeside, the remains of half-cooked meals were in the cooking pans and the men's rifles were still standing by the cabin doors. This concerned the trapper as he knew the people would not go off and leave their weapons behind. The RCMP were called in and they found the dead bodies of the sled dogs buried beneath snow drifts; they had died of hunger chained to the trees.

To this day, despite worldwide police enquiries, no sign of any of those missing has ever been found.

Fade Away

Prisoners in the Prussian prison of Weichselmunde in 1815 were kept in chains, but allowed to walk each day in the walled exercise yard. One day, everyone was surprised to see one prisoner, called Diderici, make an escape in front of them all. He literally disappeared before their eyes! Reports say that within seconds he had faded away, his manacles and ankle chains falling to the ground. He was never seen again.

A Long Trip

James Worson, a shoemaker from Leamington Spa, UK, was proud of his fitness and stamina. One day in 1873, he waged a bet with two friends that he could run to Coventry and back. The three of them set off. Worson jogged along the road and his friends followed in a horse-drawn cart. They were close behind and watching Worson carefully because they hoped he would tire and give up, so they would win the bet.

After a few miles the shoemaker was still jogging, when suddenly he stumbled, cried out, tripped forwards – and vanished! He was never seen again. Now that's what you might call a giant leap for mankind.

The painter David Hockney, the composer Olivier Messiaen and the poet Arthur Rinbaud, all have one thing in common: 'synaesthesia'. One in ten million people have this rare 'joining of the senses'. What they experience is not imaginary, but a real sensation. For example if a synaesthete were listening to music, they would also experience a taste or see a colour or shape. If looking at the colour red, they may also smell it, or if eating chicken pie might also experience a prickly sensation or hear a sound.

This makes a much more confusing world than most of us experience!

Oh baby!

On December 1st, 1992, The *Weekly World News* reported that a young mother in Holland had given birth to a very unusual baby girl. The child could reputedly vanish and reappear, even when someone was holding her. She could float in the air and crawl through walls. The child's doctor, Dr Margery Brandt, told reporters in Amsterdam, "It sounds far-fetched I know, but facts are facts."

Rain Makers

In July 1993, there was no monsoon in India, so the Government commissioned 11 days of rituals which they hoped would appease the Hindu rain god, Varuna. Within two hours of the start of the ceremonies, rain had begun to fall, and five days later it was still falling! Tragically, so much rain fell that rivers burst their banks, flooding nearly half of Bangladesh and much of India and Nepal.

In December 1916, the new 13 billion-gallon Morena Reservoir in the US was nearly empty, so San Diego councilmen decided to call in a rainmaker. For $10,000, Charles Hatfield promised to fill it before the end of the year. 1.02 inches of rain fell on the 30th December. By the end of January it was still raining and the water was flowing 1.21m (4 feet) deep over the top of the reservoir. The San Diego river burst its banks and flooded the land. Houses floated out to sea, boats were swept off their moorings, railway lines disappeared and hundreds of snakes slithered into the streets. 110 of the county's 112 bridges were washed away and the city was completely cut off for a week. Then the lower dam burst and a 15.5m wall of water crashed down into the valley.

Charles Hatfield certainly kept his promise!

Dead or Alive

In the mid 17th century, workmen were digging a ditch just outside Amritsar in northwest India when they dug so deep they disturbed a tomb. In this tomb lay the mummified body of a young yogi (holy man), dressed in faded orange robes. They removed the body from the tomb and left it on the ground. As the sun warmed it, the skin miraculously began to change and become less dry and brittle...and before long the yogi was awake and talking! Hardly had the workmen recovered from their shock, when the man told them he had been placed in the tomb over 100 years before…

Yogis and fakirs in India have the reputed ability to slow down their bodily functions. In 1835, the *Calcutta Medical Times* reported on a fakir called Haridas who made a practice of being buried alive and then being dug up again. Once he was wrapped in linen and padlocked into a chest which was then sealed with the Maharaja's personal seal. The chest was buried, crops were sown above it and a wall built around it. Guards were put on a 24 hour watch.

Forty days later, when the barley had sprouted, the chest was dug up and Haridas lay dead inside. Within an hour he was back to normal! He explained this by telling how some days before his burial he had eaten only yoghurt and milk and then fasted completely. Now that's what you'd call "having a lotta bottle!" Er...don't try this at home.

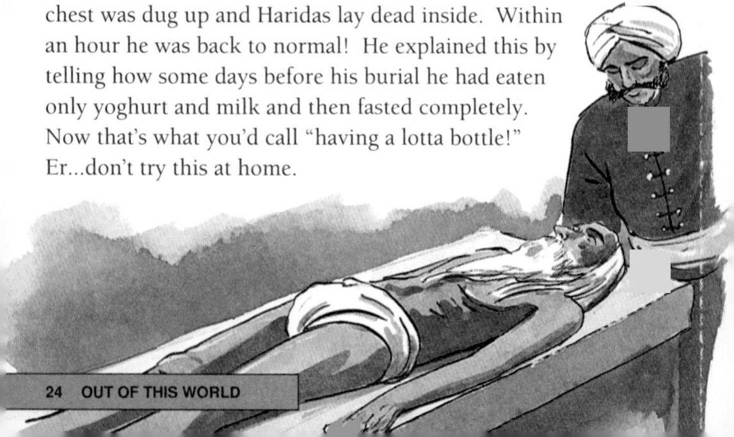

Dowsing

Dowsing is the art of finding hidden things by using a hand-held tool as a focus for the mind. The tool jumps in the dowser's hand when held over the spot where the thing is hidden. Dowsing is most often used to locate underground sources of water, oil and other minerals, often using metal rods, birch twigs or a crystal on a thread.

No one is quite sure how dowsing works. It could be that dowsers are people who are especially sensitive to minute magnetic vibrations produced by the buried substance and that these vibrations cause their arms to twitch and so move the rods. This theory however, does not explain how dowsers can dowse over a map.

In 1993, two British skiers were lost in a blizzard, 4,000 feet up in a Bavarian alp. Rescuers searched for hours but finally gave up. Temperatures were dropping below zero and it was more than likely that the climbers would die before morning.

A local man who was a dowser offered to help. Holding a thin piece of wire he dowsed over a map of the area and pinpointed a spot. The rescue team set off again and found the skiers just where the dowser had said they would be.

Remote Viewing

For more than 20 years, the US army and the CIA has trained and used people to see into other countries using just the power of their mind – their extrasensory perception (ESP). This type of spying is fast, cheap and almost untraceable.

The remote viewers are given map co-ordinates that could be anywhere in the world and asked to describe what they see at these locations. They might say, "I see lots of trees. Hidden in the trees is a building." The person working with them could ask them to describe the building. The viewer might even be able to 'go inside' the building, as if he was there, and describe what he saw.

The people chosen for the programme are not just those with strong ESP talents, but also artists, army personnel used to looking at aerial photographs and ordinary citizens. The Admiral in charge of the project believes, and has proved, that anyone can be trained to use this talent.

Many police forces today use remote viewers or clairvoyants (clear seers) to help them solve crimes or find missing people. Perhaps your mind's eye is more powerful than you think?

Telepathy

Telepathy means 'far-feeling' and is the word used to describe what happens when one mind communicates with another mind without words. It is most usually pictures or feelings which are 'picked up', not words. Most people have experienced some form of telepathy if they stop and think about it. Have you ever heard the telephone ring, and had the feeling that you know who the caller is going to be? Or perhaps you have said something to a friend who's said, "Oh! That's just what I was thinking!" Strange isn't it?

Sometimes telepathy happens just between close friends or relatives. A doctor in Connecticut, USA, recorded the case of a mother who dropped her son at his friend's house and left them to play in the swimming pool while she went to the supermarket. Halfway through her shopping she saw a sudden mental image of her son at the bottom of the pool. The feeling was so strong that she left her trolley in the middle of the supermarket, rushed to her car and drove quickly back to the friend's house. The other children there were playing in the garden. Her son was not. She ran to the pool and he was lying on the bottom at the deep end. She dived in, pulled him out and saved his life!

Precognition

Precognition (knowing beforehand) is the seeing or premonition (warning beforehand) of future events in some way. Sometimes people don't pick up any clear images or emotions consciously but they just get a nagging feeling inside.

In 1898 in America, a book called *Futility* was published. It tells the tale of a 70,000 ton liner, the Titan, which, on its first voyage across the Atlantic in the month of April, hits an iceberg and sinks, drowning most of its 2,500 passengers and crew... In April 1912, the 66,000 ton liner, the Titanic, set sail for the USA but struck an iceberg and sank, drowning most of the 2,224 passengers and crew. There would have been more people on board, but some of the passengers and crew experienced premonitions of the disaster and decided not to sail. Perhaps the writer of the novel also had a premonition?

A soldier in India was on his way down the Kyber Pass to the army club in the valley below. He hitched a lift, but halfway down felt very strongly that something was going to go wrong and asked the lorry driver to stop and let him off. Another lorry came along and he hitched a ride on that. About a mile further on they found the first lorry had fallen over the side of a ravine.

Mind-Reader

Here's a mind-reading game you can play with your friends. Who knows, it may help you to develop your powers of concentration...

Copy these drawings on to small pieces of card, perhaps add some more shapes of your own to make the game last even longer.

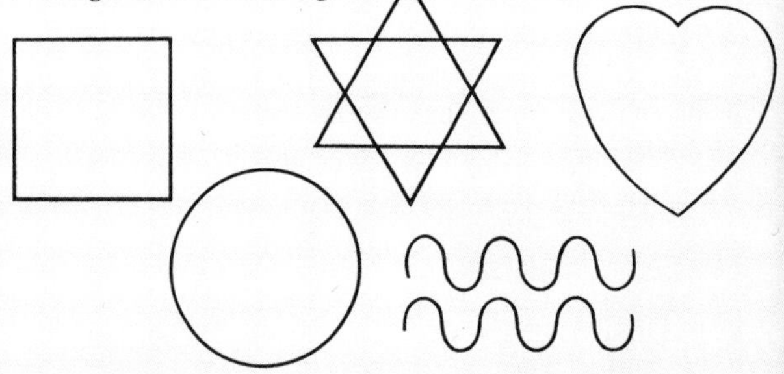

1. Give each of your friends a piece of paper and a pencil.
2. Ask them to sit on the other side of the room you are in, with their backs to you.
3. Now, shuffle the cards, and take one out at random.
4. Look at the card you have chosen and concentrate hard on it.
5. Try to 'send' the picture you can see to your friends.
6. Agree amongst yourselves beforehand how long you will do this for: about 5 minutes should be enough.
7. During this time your friends should also concentrate hard on trying to pick up the image you have in your mind's eye.
8. Ask them to draw what they see on the piece of paper, and when time's up, compare your results.

You might be surprised at how your minds can work!

Sweet Dreams

Dreams are a bit like codes or puzzles. Many of the dream pictures we have are symbols for something else. You may dream you are eating a large marshmallow that is bigger than your face (yum!), and then wake up with your head under the pillow. Very disappointing!

One lady dreamt that she was walking along a road and a baby sparrow was walking beside her, dragging its wing on the ground. The next day she was called to go to hospital with her young son because he had broken his elbow while playing at school.

The writer Robert Louis Stevenson wrote many of his books as a result of his dreams. He was able to go to sleep and pick up a dream story where he had left off the night before.

Most people have about five dreams a night, although they will not always remember them.

Dream Diary

One way to remember your dreams, and so see if any of them come true or perhaps have a hidden message, is to:

- say to yourself as you go to sleep : "I will remember my dreams tonight."
- keep a notebook and pencil by your bed or under your pillow, and as soon as you wake up, write down all you can remember of your dream.

Marvels...

Shark sightings in Suva Harbour are very rare. In December 1992, the body of Fijian president, Ratu Sir Penaia Ganilau, who was said to be a direct descendent of the shark god Dakuwaqa, was being taken to his home on the island of Taveuni. As the funeral boat sailed out of the harbour, a school of sharks surfaced and accompanied the president on his last journey.

Captain Joseph Belain of the U.S. Army dedicated his life to save the carrier pigeon from extermination. During his burial service in the church of Gay Head, USA, a carrier pigeon flew in from the sea and sat on his coffin until the service was over.

...and Miracles

Empress Eugenie, the wife of Emperor Napoleon III, was looking for her son's grave deep in the African jungle. For days she and her friends searched dense undergrowth without success. Suddenly Eugenie cried, "Par ici! C'est la route!" and rushed off at high speed through grass higher than her head. Her friends followed her and found her clearing jungle growth from a grave marker. She claimed she had been led there, by the scent of violets, her son's favourite perfume.

In 1878, three young children were orphaned by the death of their mother and sent to live at the Orphanage and Convalescent Home at Aberlour, Scotland.
One night, the Reverend Jupp, who ran the orphanage, gave his room to some visitors and slept in with some of the children. In the night he woke to see a small cloud of light hovering over the bed of a little boy, the youngest of the three children. In the morning, as he was dressing the little boy, the child looked up at him and said, "Oh, Mr Jupp, my mother came to me last night. Did you see her?"

Shape Shifters

Have you read the book *Alice in Wonderland*? If you have, you will know that when Alice was in Wonderland she ate and drank things that made her grow and shrink. Some people claim to be able to change their body shape and size without outside help. The power to do this is one of the eight magical powers that Indian yogis strive to attain.

The Long and the Short

In the 1400s, there was reported to be a rather plump Italian nun who, every Friday, could apparently change shape and become long and thin. And if you thought that was a bit odd...

In 1878, a teenage girl in Nova Scotia woke up one morning to a sound "like thunderclaps" in time to see her sister Esther, aged 19, growing longer and taller before her eyes. This only lasted a short while and then Esther changed back to normal!

The Mark of the Cross

Some very religious Christians have been known to develop marks on their hands, feet and foreheads, which they believe are copies of Christ's wounds on the cross and which are, therefore, signs of holiness. These special marks are called 'stigmata'.

Werewolves

We all know the fairytale of Little Red Riding Hood who met a wolf pretending to be her grandmother. Folklore is full of tales of werewolves – people who can turn into wolves and then turn back into people again. Movie makers have made lots of films based on this, now almost mythical creature. But where did the myth begin?

In 1508, a German priest, Dr Johann Geiler, preached a series of sermons about werewolves in Strasbourg. In 1925, a whole village near Strasbourg, France, claimed that a local boy was a werewolf, and in 1946, an American Navajo Indian reservation was thought to have been terrorised by a werewolf. These howlers of history are hard to believe, but legend has it that the only way to kill a werewolf is with a silver bullet.

Nowadays, psychiatrists use the term "lycanthropy" to describe the condition of a patient who suffers from the delusion that he is a wolf. So perhaps it's all a figment of the imagination after all?

Black Cats and Bogeymen

Superstitions are actions linked to ideas that are based on long ago beliefs about the world we live in. Do you know any of these?

SALT: If you spill salt, throw a pinch of it over your left shoulder. It was believed that evil spirits lurked on the left side of people and that salt blinded them and stopped them working their evil.

MOTHS: If a moth flutters around you and won't go away, it is a sign that you are about to receive a letter.

WOODEN SPOONS: It is meant to be lucky for a bride to receive a wooden spoon on her wedding day.

SPIDERS: Small spiders, often called money spinners, are meant to bring good luck. You must throw them over your left shoulder first though. Not very lucky for the spider!

SILVER COIN: 'Something old, Something new, Something borrowed, And a silver sixpence in your shoe.' This old saying was considered good advice for a bride on the morning of her wedding, and is sometimes still said today. A silver coin worn in your left shoe is said to bring good luck.

ROOKS: If there are rooks nesting near your house, it is said to be a sign of good luck.

MIRROR: Breaking a mirror is meant to bring bad luck for seven years. To break the curse you are supposed to take the broken pieces and either bury them in earth or throw them into a river or stream (not very environmentally friendly!)

Number Thirteen

Thirteen is supposedly an unlucky number.

This may have evolved from there being thirteen present at Christ's Last Supper.

Have you ever noticed that there is no seat numbered 13 on most aeroplanes?

The thirteenth Apollo mission, launched from pad 39 (13 x 3) at 13.13 hours on 13th April, 1970, had so many mishaps it had to be stopped.

Friday 13th is an unlucky day. The worst day of all to be married is Friday 13th May.

Fear of the number 13 is called 'triskaidekaphobia'.

Oracles

No one can really tell your future or your fate because everything you do and every decision you make in life changes the pattern and the possibilities. Oracles are people or objects which can be used to point your attention to some of these possibilities and so give you a chance to make decisions. They have been used throughout history.

The way in which these oracles work has not yet been discovered but somehow they, or the person using them, can tune in to what is going on deep in a person's subconscious mind by the same process in which an experienced dice thrower seems to be able to affect the dice he or she is throwing.

Different people in different cultures use different objects as oracles. Whatever is used acts as a focus for the mind to concentrate on and so allows for a deeper insight than normal.

Palmistry

Palmistry is the term used to describe reading the hand. A good palmist will not try to tell your fortune but just things about you that he or she can see in the lines and shapes.

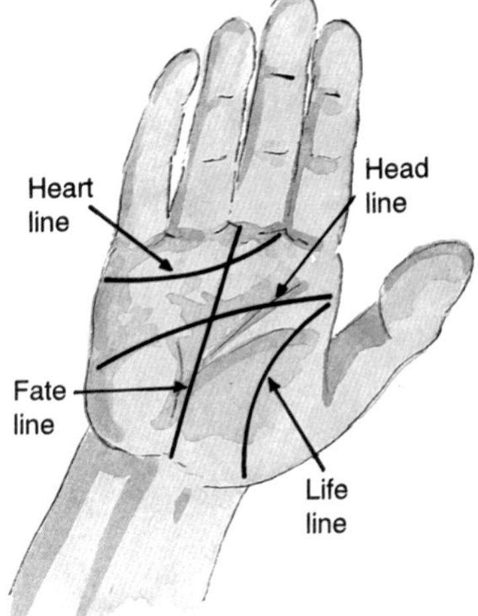

For example: did you know that the shape of your hand indicates whether you are a practical person or a thinking person? The length of your fingers might show that you are artistic and the thickness of your thumb whether you have a bad temper or not! Little lines and marks can show if you might be likely to get a certain illness, and the overall pattern of lines shows what sort of temperament you have – fiery or calm, and so on.

This picture of yourself can be useful.
For example: a man might paint pictures as a hobby but work in an office and not really like it. If a palmist tells him his hand shows strong creativity and practical business sense, this might give him the confidence to try and sell some of his paintings, which in turn might lead to him making enough money from painting to be able to leave his job and work as a painter.

Fairy Tales

Throughout history, people have talked about fairy rings and magic circles that dot the countryside. These rings are seasonally marked by a ring of mushrooms. In some parts of Britain there are still little hills and pieces of land that are set aside for the Little People. Farmers will plough right up to them but not on them, and often will not walk there either!

In 1991, on the 12th and 13th May, 930 school children at a school in Malaysia reported seeing hundreds of tiny people coming out of a hole near the drain of a housing estate. The little folk were dressed in red and were about 6 cm high. Some were also seen near a hole at the foot of a tree. One boy reportedly tried to catch one but it stabbed his hand, leaving a tiny mark and a bruise.

In 1935, a girl working in County Mayo, Ireland, was sent on an errand to the next village. On the way she passed by a hill with a fairy ring of trees on its top. She climbed up the hill to look at the view – and found she couldn't get out of the ring of trees. Every time she tried she was jerked back by an invisible wall. She was there so long that search parties set out to look for her and one came right up to the edge of the ring. She called and waved but they neither saw her nor heard her. Many hours later she found the invisible barrier had gone and she was able to hurry home.

Corn Circle Phenomena

Over the past ten years or more, circles and other shapes have been mysteriously appearing in fields of many types of crop. They have also appeared on the surface of swamps and frozen snow and the tops of dense forests. In Britain they seem to appear mainly within the southern area, from Vantage, Oxfordshire, to Winchester, to Warminster and Wiltshire, but the circles and very complex patterns appear in at least twenty six other countries and continents, and the list continues to grow!

Some claims were made in the newspapers that the circles were hoaxes made by two men known as Doug and Dave. However, Doug and Dave would have to be a phenomena in themselves if they hoaxed all the circles that appear, not just here, but all over the world.

Corn Circle Phenomena

These circles and shapes, or pictograms as they are now called, have certain things in common:

- There are no footmarks or signs of approach around them.
- The stems of the crops are bent not broken (as in the hoaxes) into a swirl and at an angle at which crops such as wheat would normally snap.
- The growth nodes on the stem of the crop are damaged as if the water in the cellular tissue has boiled.
- A strong energy field exists within the pictograms, which can be detected by instruments and by dowsers.

Some people even report experiencing strange tingling or buzzing sensations inside a pictogram.

Signs and Wonders

Throughout history many things, such as beads, frogs and fish, have reportedly fallen from the sky. Experts usually explain these strange showers away by saying that a whirlwind picked them up and then dropped them.

In 1897, seeds fell on several towns in the Italian province of Macerata, and the 18th September issue of *Notes and Queries* identified the seeds as those of the Judas tree, in the first stage of germination. The Judas tree only grows in Central Africa!

Weeping Statues

How can a stone statue shed real tears? Unbelievable it may be, but here are some interesting details:

- It is recorded that a statue of Apollo once wept for three days and nights.

- A 16 inch (40 cm) crucifix in Walthamstow, London, was seen to shed tears on at least 30 different days between May and July 1966.

- During 1719 in Syracuse, Sicily, a marble statue of St Lucy wept continuously while the town was under siege.

Footprints in the Dark

On the morning of February 9th, 1855, the folk of South Devon woke to find it had snowed during the night. Snow lay deep on the ground, and on the tops of trees, walls and roofs – and someone, or something, had walked in it – along the ground, up the walls, over the roofs, in gardens and in courtyards enclosed by high fences. Strange footprints were everywhere!

They looked like long, hooved footprints, evenly spaced at 8 inches (21 cm) and placed one in front of another as a man, not an animal, would walk, but in places that no man could walk. For one hundred miles or more the trail of hooved footprints stretched ahead. At one point they jumped the two mile wide estuary of the River Exe and carried on. At another they passed one on each side of a haystack and again on each side of a 14 ft (4.26 m) high wall.

Similar footprints have been found in other parts of the world and at other times in history, but no one has yet solved the mystery of who or what made them.

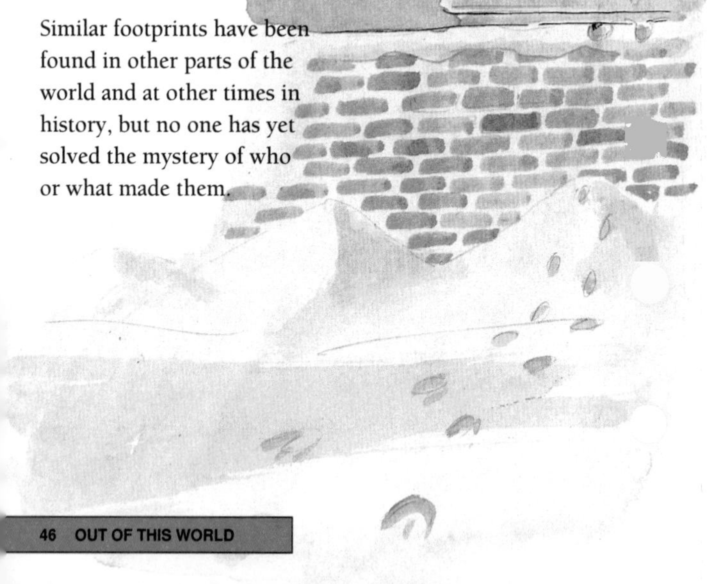

Signs and Wonders

The Parisien churchyard of Saint-Medard was the scene of many miracles for six years.

It all started when the Deacon of Paris, who was famous as a healer, was buried in May 1727. At the funeral, a crippled boy was suddenly found to be healed. His withered leg became whole and strong. News of this miracle spread and soon lepers, and people with all sorts of handicaps, were rushing to be healed.

Learned books were written about what was going on at the churchyard, but no one could find an explanation. In the end, so many people were turning up there, either to be healed or just to watch the miracles, that the local council closed it down in 1732.

Call it Coincidence...

Jennifer Roberts was camping in Australia with her husband. She was looking at the cover of a novel, which showed a man being struck by lightning, when suddenly she too was struck by lightning!

A couple were driving south one day and stopped at a layby to rest. Another car pulled in and the two couples got talking. The man in the second car mentioned that he had lost his wallet six months before but someone had handed it in to the police station with nothing missing. He took it out to show the first couple and the wife recognised it as the one she had found when on holiday and handed to the police.

Noel McCabe was listening to a record, 'Cry of the Wild Goose', when a Canada goose crashed through his window. Enough to give anyone goosebumps!